The Hopes and Dreams Series
Irish-Americans

Hungry
No More

A story based on history

Second Edition

Tana Reiff

Illustrations by Tyler Stiene

PRO LINGUA ASSOCIATES

Pro Lingua Associates, Publishers

P.O. Box 1348
Brattleboro, Vermont 05302-1348 USA
Office: 802 257 7779
Orders: 800 366 4775
E-mail: orders@ProLinguaAssociates.com
SAN: 216-0579
Webstore: www.ProLinguaAssociates.com

Copyright © 2016 by Tana Reiff

Text ISBN 13: 978-0-86647-420-7; 10: 0-86647-420-X
Audio CD ISBN 13: 978-0-86647-421-4; 10: 0-86647-421-8

The first edition of this book was originally published by Fearon Education, a
division of David S. Lake Publishers, Belmont, California, Copyright © 1989, later
by Pearson Education. This, the second edition, has been revised and redesigned.

The cover and illustrations are by Tyler Stiene. The book was set and designed by
Tana Reiff, consulting with A.A. Burrows, using the Adobe *Century Schoolbook*
typeface for the text. This is a digital adaptation of one of the most popular faces
of the twentieth century. Century's distinctive roman and italic fonts and its clear,
dark strokes and serifs were designed, as the name suggests, to make schoolbooks
easy to read. The display font used on the cover and titles is a 21st-century digital
invention titled Telugu. It is designed to work on all digital platforms and with Indic
scripts. Telugu is named for the Telugu people in southern India and their widely
spoken language. This is a simple, strong, and interesting sans serif display font.

This book was printed and bound by KC Book Manufacturing in North Kansas City,
Missouri. Printed in the United States. Second edition 2016

The Hopes and Dreams Series
by Tana Reiff

The Magic Paper (Mexican-Americans)
For Gold and Blood (Chinese-Americans)
Nobody Knows (African-Americans)
Little Italy (Italian-Americans)
Hungry No More (Irish-Americans)
Sent Away (Japanese-Americans)
Two Hearts (Greek-Americans)

Contents

1 The Old Days 1

2 Potato Problems 5

3 Leaving Ireland 12

4 Greenhorns in America ... 16

5 Hard Work 22

6 Blasting Rock 27

7 Boston Life 32

8 The Church 39

9 Going to War 44

10 No Irish Need Apply 48

11 Taking Care 52

12 News 56

13 War Is Over 60

Glossary 67

1 The Old Days
Galway, Ireland, 1845

The story ended.
Everyone laughed.

"Those were
the good old days,"
said Father Patrick.
"I was young then
and you were children."

"You are still
young at heart,"
Johnny McGee
said to the priest.

"Tell us more!"
said Mary McGee.
"I like to hear
your stories
when you visit."
She was holding
her son Little John
on her lap.

"Yes, yes,"
said the old priest.
"Those were better days
in beautiful, green Ireland.
Every family
kept chickens
and a pig.
They sold eggs.
And when the pig
was fat enough,
they ate its meat.
They used every part
of that pig.
Life was not easy,
but we were never hungry."

"But now ..."
Johnny looked down.
"Now there is
only the potato."

"Only the potato,"
Father Patrick repeated.
"However,
the potato is good!
Boil a few potatoes
in a big pot
over the fire
and that is dinner!"

Johnny knew
all about potatoes.
He and Mary
paid rent for land
to farm potatoes.
They worked very hard
and grew lots of potatoes.
Year after year,
the potatoes grew.

They were poor,
but they had potatoes.
The McGee family
ate potatoes
every day of the week.
The potato
was everything
in Ireland.

"Thank God
for potatoes!"
said Mary McGee.
"What would we do
without potatoes?"

"Amen,"
said Father Patrick.
"And have you heard
about old Mrs. Cleary?"

"Tell us!"
Mary begged him.
"You know
what everyone is doing!"

And Father Patrick
carried on.

2 Potato Problems

Each year,
Johnny and Mary
saved small potatoes.
In spring
they planted them
in the ground.
Before long,
green potato sprouts
popped up.

But one day
Johnny saw trouble.
The potato leaves
had black spots
all over them.

Johnny talked
to the other farmers.
They too were seeing
black spots.

Father Patrick
came to visit
that night.
"Everyone around here
has black potato plants,"
he said.
"I hear
it's a blight.
The plants
are rotting!
The potato crop
could fail!
People are afraid."

"We can get by,"
said Mary.
"We have enough potatoes
from last year.
We can get through
one bad year."

And it was
a bad year.
The potato crop failed.
The blight
took everything.

The McGees got
no potatoes at all.

The potatoes
from last year
were not enough
to feed the family.
And they had to save some
to plant next year.
Johnny and Mary
were hungry,
and Little John cried
almost all the time.
They gave him
any real food
they could get.
They pretended
to eat with him.
When he wasn't looking,
they ate weeds
so their son
could have enough.
It was the only way
for them
to stay alive.

"Next year
will be better,"
Mary kept saying.

Johnny was glad
when planting time
came again.
There was hope
in the spring fields.
He and Mary
planted the little potatoes
they had saved.
Johnny watched
as the new shoots
came up in rows.
"It is good
to see green again,"
he said to Mary.

Johnny checked
the potatoes
every day.
One day
the plants were green.

The next day
they had a few spots.
The day after that,
they were black.

Johnny's heart
was heavy
when he told Mary
the bad news.

"What shall we do?"
Mary asked.
"We have
no old potatoes
to fall back on!"

"We are not
the only ones,"
said Johnny sadly.
"All of Ireland
is in trouble."

For a short time,
England sent wheat
to Ireland.
"I'm glad

to have this wheat,"
said Mary.
"But we get
so little of it.
It doesn't last long."

And then
wheat from England
stopped coming.
Everyone was hungry.
People starved to death.
Some people
left for England,
Canada, and America.
People lay dead
by the side of the road.
Old Mrs. Cleary
stayed in her cottage.
All she could do
was wait to die.

"We are so hungry,"
Mary told Father Patrick.
"We worry
about our son.
We might die
just like the others.

Then what would become
of Little John?
What shall we do?"

"Keep the faith,
my children.
Please don't leave Ireland,"
begged the priest.
"Things will get better.
We must keep praying
that the potatoes
will come back."

3 Leaving Ireland

"I'm sorry, Father,"
said Johnny
to the priest.
"Things are very bad —
gone too far.
Our mother country England
is not helping us.
If we stay in Ireland,
we will surely die.
We must think about
our little son.
There is nothing left
for us to eat.
We cannot wait
another year.
We are young.
We must get away.
We will go
to America."

"I understand,"
said Father Patrick.

"But did you know
it costs less
to go to Canada?
Some people walk
from Canada to America."

"What a long walk
that would be!"
said Johnny.
"We are not as strong
as we once were.
It would be better
to go to America.
The American ships
are better, too.
And an American ship
will take us
straight to Boston."

So Johnny and Mary
did not pay their rent.
They used the money
to pay for their trip.
Money could not buy food.
But it could buy escape.

Father Patrick
saw them off.

"You have my blessing,"
he said.
He hugged each one
and patted them
on the head.
"God be with you."

The McGee family
went to Liverpool, England,
across the Irish Sea.
Some Irish people
stayed in Liverpool.
But the McGees
boarded a ship.
It carried animals
as well as people.
Animal noises
followed them down
under the ship's deck.
Cows.
Pigs.
Goats.
Even geese.
The animal smells
and the salt air
stayed in their noses
all the way to Boston.

The McGees were three
of 125 people
on that ship.
They made friends
with a young man
named Kennedy.
His family's farm
in Ireland
was not big enough.
One son
had to leave.
Kennedy lost
a coin toss.
He was the one
to go to America.
Everyone on the ship
had a story.
But Kennedy
told funny stories
that helped people
pass the time.

In 40 days
and 40 nights
the McGecs
set foot in America.

4 Greenhorns in America

Johnny and Mary
stepped off the ship.

A man called out,
"Welcome to Boston!"

"Thank you!"
said Johnny.
"You talk
like someone from Ireland!"

"That's right!"
said the man.
"I'm here
to help you greenhorns.
Need a place to live?
I can find it.
Need jobs?
I know
where the jobs are.
How can I help?"

"We need work,"
said Johnny.

"But first, we need
a room.
We don't know
if we will stay
in Boston.
We might move on."

"You will stay
in the city!"
laughed the man.
"Why go out
to the country?
The land
was no friend to you
back in Ireland,
now, was it?"

"No, no, it wasn't,"
said Mary softly.

"I will put you
in a good room
in East Boston,"
said the man.
"Lots of Irish there.
What do you say,
Mr. —"

"McGee,"
said Johnny.
He put out his hand.
"Johnny McGee.
And this is
my wife, Mary."

"Name's McNair,"
said the man.
He shook Johnny's hand.
He looked at Mary.
She was holding Little John
in her arms.
"Now isn't that
a fine-looking lad
you've got there!"

Mary smiled
for the first time
in a long time.
She loved
her little boy.
Every night,
she prayed
for more children.

McNair kept talking.
"Johnny McGee,
you are a big man.
You can work
on the railroad.
The work is hard.
But the pay is good.
Fair is fair,
I always say.
And you, Mary.
You can work
in the wool mill.
There is work
for everyone
here in America!"

McNair took the McGees
to their room
in East Boston.
He got jobs
for both of them,
He told them
about a woman nearby.
For a little money,
she took care of children
while parents worked.

Then McNair
asked for money.
"I like to help people,"
he said.
"But I have to make a living!"

Johnny handed him
the money.

"Good luck!"
said McNair.
He waved
as he walked away.
"God be with you,
you two greenhorns!"

After McNair left,
Johnny turned to Mary.
"Did that seem
like a lot of money?"

"Yes, Johnny,
it did,"
said Mary.
"But what else
could we do?
We need help
in a new country.

We don't know anyone.
He was there
to help us."

"But I did not think
an Irishman
would do this
to other Irish,"
said Johnny sadly.

"Maybe someday
it won't seem
like a lot of money,"
Mary smiled.
"We will work.
We will have money.
We will have
enough food to eat
every day of the week.
We will be
strong again."

"We will take care
of ourselves,"
Johnny added.
"And we will be
hungry no more."

5 Hard Work

Johnny was away
for months at a time.
There was a railroad
to build
through the mountains
of Vermont.
Johnny McGee
helped to build it.

The work
was back-breaking.
To Johnny,
it was harder
than farming.
Johnny was given
a pick and a shovel.
He dug into the earth
to make
the railroad bed.
He laid rails
onto the bed.
He drove spikes
into the rails.

Johnny started working
when the sun came up.
He did not stop
until the sun
went down.

Blasting large rocks
was the worst work of all.
More than once,
he saw his friends
get blown up
along with the rocks.

For all his work,
Johnny's pay
was 25 dollars a month.
But sometimes
the boss
kept the money
for himself.
Some months,
Johnny never saw
a penny.

Back in the city
Mary worked
at the wool mill.

She ran a machine.
The machine
spun wool.
The mill
was hot and dirty.
And very noisy.
The wool
hurt Mary's skin.

There was
a bright side
to Mary's job.
She made friends
at the mill.
And she made money.
It wasn't much.
She was paid
even less than Johnny.
But she was thankful.
The money
that she and Johnny made
paid the rent.
It paid the lady
who watched Little John.
It put food
on the table.

Johnny came home
every few months.
Mary was so happy
to see him.
Their time together
was very special.

"Life is not easy,"
Johnny said one night.
"We work so hard.
We can't be together
all the time.
I miss you and Little John
when I'm away."

"Look at this table,"
said Mary.
"We have food.
Not just potatoes!
We have meat, too!
And right now
we are together.
I am so very thankful
for what we have."

"You are right,"
said Johnny.
"We have much
to be thankful for.
We have not had
one hungry day
in our new life."

"Father Patrick
would be happy for us,"
said Mary.

But she and Johnny
would never know
whether Father Patrick
had enough to eat.
They wrote letters
to their old priest
across the ocean.
They never got
a letter in return.

6 Blasting Rock

Back at work,
there was rock to blast.
The men drilled holes
into the rock.
It was very hard work.
Johnny started singing.

Drill, ye tarriers, drill
For it's work all day
For the sugar in your tea
Down beyond the railway
And drill, ye tarriers, drill!
And blast! And fire!

"Sing along with me!"
he called out.
The other men
joined in.
The drilling work
seemed to go faster
when they sang.

The boss saw
what Johnny was doing.
How he worked hard.
How he did things right.
How he got
the other workers
to keep moving.
How he kept everyone
singing and working
at the same time.
The boss also heard
Johnny speaking English.

So when the boss left,
Johnny became the new boss.
The company
started paying him more.
Now he was the leader
of the group.

"Keep an eye
on McGee,"
a worker named Murphy
whispered to the others.
"The old boss
took our money.
So will McGee."

That talk
got back to Johnny,
and he didn't like it.

"I would never
take your money,"
Johnny told the men.
"I am not
that kind of boss.
You can be sure of that,
my friends."

Still, Murphy
kept his eye
on Johnny.
Months went by.
Johnny never took a penny.

One day Murphy said,
"Johnny McGee,
you are a good boss.
You make people work.
But you pay us
what we earn.
You are a fair man,
Johnny McGee."

From that day on,
Johnny and Murphy
were friends.
Murphy became
Johnny's right-hand man.
Johnny knew
he could count on Murphy.

"Tomorrow
we'll have a big rock
to blow up,"
Murphy told Johnny.
"We should take turns
setting up the blast.
I'll go first."

All the holes
in the rock
had been drilled.
Murphy put black powder
into each hole.
He stuck a fuse, or cord,
into the black powder.
He covered that
with sand.
He packed down the sand
with an iron pole.

But it all went wrong.
The iron pole
hit the rock.
It made a spark
that set off
the black powder.
Rock and dust
blew up
toward the sky.
The earth shook.

Then it was over.
A huge cloud
of broken rocks
fell back down to earth.

"Where's Murphy?"
Johnny shouted.
He looked around.
"Murphy!
Where are you?"

It was too late.
Murphy lay
under a pile of rocks.
He was dead.

7 Boston Life

Johnny was still sad
about Murphy
when he headed to Boston
a few weeks later.
But he was so happy
to see Mary and Little John.
He picked up Mary
and swung her around.

"I have a surprise!"
said Mary.

"No need to tell me,"
said Johnny.
"I can see!
There is a new baby
on the way!"

"I had to quit work,"
said Mary.
"But now
I can keep Little John
at home with me."

"I want to stay
in Boston,"
said Johnny.
"I want to be here
for our family.
I can find work here."

So Johnny
began to work
for the city.
He got a job
as a policeman.
"I couldn't help Murphy,"
he said.
"But maybe
I can help
other people."

A few months later
the baby was born.
"We will name him
Patrick Murphy McGee,"
Johnny said.
"After your father
and Father Patrick
and my friend Murphy.
We'll call him Paddy."

Life in the city
was new to Johnny.
Until now,
he had not seen much of it.
Some families
lived in tiny shacks
made of old boards.
People begged for money
in the street.
There were fires
nearly every day.
Many people
had no place to live.
Many got sick
and died.

So Johnny and Mary
felt lucky.
They didn't have much.
Their home
was one small room
in a run-down building.
In the room
were a bed,
two chairs,
a black stove,
and an iron tub.

Nothing more.
But they had a roof
over their heads.
They had work.
They had food.
Life was surely not easy.
But it was better here
than in Ireland.

Across the hall
lived a group
of young men.
What a surprise
that one of them
was Kennedy
from the ship!

The lads
went to the pub
every night.
Kennedy told stories.
They all drank
and had a good time.
They almost never
went to church.

Johnny was different.
He and Mary

went to mass
every Sunday.
They played
by the rules.
A man like Johnny
stayed away
from the pub.

  "I want to help people
in every way I can,"
Johnny said to Mary
one day.
So he became
a volunteer firefighter.
He joined
a group of men
who put out fires
without being paid.
When the bell went off,
Johnny took his coat
off the hook
and ran.

  Sometimes
two volunteer groups
would show up
at the same fire.
Both groups wanted

to put out the fire.
A fight
would break out
between the groups.
Sometimes
a house burned
to the ground
while the men fought.

"This is silly,"
Johnny said one day.
"Each group
should fight fires
in their own part
of town."

"You are
a good leader,"
a Boston leader
told Johnny.
"You should become
a ward heeler."

And so he did.
As a ward heeler,
Johnny found jobs
for new people.

He got people
out of jail.
He sent flowers
when someone died.
Johnny was doing
what he wanted to do.
He was helping people.
He got paid
to be a policeman.
But he also
was a firefighter
and a ward heeler,
for no pay.

Another baby
was on the way.
The McGee family
moved to a bigger place.
Now they had two rooms
instead of just one.

For the next five years
there was a new baby
each year.
After eight children,
the McGees
moved again.

8 The Church

More and more Irish people
came to America.
Most of them
came to Boston or New York.
Some Americans
were not happy about it.

"The Irish
are taking our jobs!"
they said.
"They are lazy!
They drink
on Saturday night!
They are Catholic!
Down with the Irish!"

Fights broke out.
The police
had to break them up.
The Americans
did not like
Irish policemen.

They called
all Irish people
"Paddy" or "Biddy."
Johnny didn't like it.
It was mean.
And besides,
Paddy was
his son Patrick's nickname.
Biddy was
his daughter Bridget's nickname.

"The Boston mothers
won't let their children
play with our children,"
Mary told Johnny.
"Two of our Bridget's friends
stopped speaking to her.
What should we do?"

"Let it be,"
said Johnny.
"We don't want
to set off sparks.
Keep our children
with other Irish children.
We don't want them
to get hurt.

Let them play
in the church yard.
They will be safe there."

In the summer
the eight McGee children
played outside
every day.
One hot day
they were playing
in the church yard.
They ran
round and round
among the stones and flowers.
They played
silly games.

Suddenly
a mob of men
stormed into the yard.
They called out
bad names.
They waved sticks
in the air.
The children cried.

"Go away!"
called the men.
"You, Paddy!
You, Biddy!
Get out of here!
We do not want
to hurt you!"

The mob ran
inside the church.
The children hid
behind the gravestones
in the yard.
They heard the sound
of breaking wood inside.
They heard the crash
of stone falling
to the floor.
The children
were afraid to move.

Then they heard
the church door
bang shut.
Everything got quiet.
The men were gone.

The children
walked slowly
into the church.
It was a mess.
Wood and stone
lay in pieces.
It was an ugly sight.

"We must go home,"
Bridget told the others.
"We must tell our Mam
what we saw."

9 Going to War

"Why did those men
do such a mean thing?"
Bridget asked her Mam.
"They broke our church!"

"What you saw
was hate,"
explained Mary McGee.
"Hate is bad.
Some people
hate the Irish
and our church.
We must not hate anyone.
We must not hurt anyone.
Never be so angry.
Pray for love instead."

Mary and Johnny
helped to fix the church.
They and their friends
gave money.
They made new seats.
They cut new stone.

It took a year.
But now the church
looked like new.
They never found out
who made the mess.

Then it was time
to get ready for war.
It was
the Civil War
in America.
The North and South
were fighting each other.
The North wanted
to free the slaves.
The South did not.

"I don't want
to free the slaves,"
Johnny said.

"Why not?"
asked Bridget.

"I am afraid
they will take our jobs,"
said her father.

"Do you hate
the slaves?"
asked the little girl.

"No,"
Johnny said.
"But the Irish
have a hard enough time.
We need our jobs."

"Then why
must you fight
in the war?"
asked Bridget.
"Mam told me
not to hate.
She said
not to hurt anyone."

"We have no choice.
We must fight
to save the Union!"
Johnny explained.

So Johnny
helped put together
a volunteer unit.

Together,
they would become
soldiers in the Civil War.
He tried
to find Kennedy
and his friends.
He found
only Kennedy's wife
and children.
Kennedy had gotten sick
and died young.
His children
would have to carry on
without him.

But Johnny
found other men.
Each man
carried his own gun.
And each man
learned how to use it.
Before long,
the group was ready.
They joined
the Irish Brigade
and marched off to war.

10 No Irish Need Apply

Once again
Mary was home
without her husband.
This time
she had eight children
to take care of.
The older children
helped with the younger ones.
But Mary was in charge.
And once again,
the family
needed money.

"I must find work,"
Mary told the children.
"Go get me
a newspaper.
I will find out
who needs help."

She read
help-wanted ads
in the paper.

WANTED:
Girl of neat habits
and kind heart
to take charge
of two small children.
No Irish need apply.

WANTED:
An American woman
to do the housework
of a small family.
No Irish need apply.

HOUSEMAID NEEDED:
Work all around the house.
No Irish need apply.

"What shall I do?"
Mary wondered.
No one wanted
an Irish woman.

Mary did not give up.
The help-wanted ads
included addresses.
"I'll just show them
who I am,"
she said to herself.

She picked up
the newspaper.
She slammed the door
on her way out.

  She found
the first address
that she looked for.
She knocked
on the door.
A woman
opened the door.
"May I help you?"
she asked Mary.

  "I see
that you need help,"
said Mary.
"I know
how to clean.
I know
how to take care
of children.
My husband
is off at war.
I will do
very good work.
May I have the job?"

The woman
looked Mary over.
"You seem clean enough,"
she said.
"My name
is Mrs. Brock.
Come in."

The woman
never asked Mary
if she was Irish.
"I need someone
right away,"
she said.
"When can you start?"

11 Taking Care

Every morning
Mary woke up
before the sun came up.
Every morning
she walked to work.
The Brock family lived
three miles across town.

Mary cleaned
the Brock house.
She cooked
for the Brock family.
She took care
of three Brock children.

She got home
after the sun went down.
Then she cleaned
her own family's three rooms.
She cooked
for her own family.
She took care
of her own eight children.

And always,
all the time,
her Johnny
was on her mind.
She felt afraid.
Johnny was a brave man.
But even brave men
die in wars.

Every now and then
a letter came
from Johnny.
Sometimes the letters
were many months old.
Perhaps Johnny
was still all right
months ago,
but Mary
could not know
if another letter
was on its way.

She read
each letter
out loud
to the children.

"My dear family,"
wrote Johnny.
"I am in Virginia.
The Battle of Bull Run
ended yesterday.
We marched
into battle.
We waved
the green flag
of the Irish Brigade.
It is showing wear.
We lost that battle.
But don't let
anyone tell you
the Irish
are afraid to fight.
We are brave.
We fight hard.
We have lost many men
in this war.
My friend
lost a leg
for the North.
I am all right.
Do not worry.
I will be home soon."

Mary held the letter
close to her heart.
"He will come home,"
she said to herself.
"My Johnny McGee
will come home.
I keep the faith
that he will."

12 News

"Still another man
from Boston
has been killed
in the war!"
said Mr. Brock.

"Oh, how sad!"
said Mary.
"Did the man
have a family?"

"I believe so,"
said Mr. Brock.
"They live
over on Union Street."

"Oh, the poor family,"
said Mary.
She knew
that Union Street
was an Irish part of town.
She could not say
what was on her mind.

She felt so thankful
that the dead man
was not Johnny.
She said a little prayer
for the family
on Union Street.

"The war
cannot last long,"
Mr. Brock added.
"The South
is finished.
They will give up.
It's a matter of time."
He looked
toward the window.
"Do you hear
that noise outside?"
he asked Mary.

Mr. Brock
opened the front door.
He stepped out
into the street.

Mary did not think
about the noise.

She could think
only of her husband.
On her hands and knees,
she was washing
the kitchen floor.
She heard his name
in every push
of the rag.
Johnny.
Johnny.
Johnny.

    Suddenly
Mr. Brock
came running
into the house.
He ran
into the kitchen.
His face
was one big smile.
"Good news, Mary!"
he shouted.
"The war is over!
Our men
are on their way home!"

The wet rag
fell from Mary's hands.
She held
her hands together
and looked
toward the sky.
"Oh, thank God!
Please may my Johnny
be safe!"

13 The War Is Over

Weeks went by
after Mr. Brock's news.
There was no word
from Johnny.
Maybe he was
on his way home.
Maybe he was hurt.
Or maybe …
Mary did not want
to think about it.

None of the Irish Brigade
had come home yet.
There was no news.
Only waiting.

Then one day
Mary was walking home
from the Brocks' house.
The sun was low.

The sky
was almost dark.
The air
was cool.
Everything was quiet.
Then Mary heard
the soft beat
of a drum.
The sound
was coming
from far up the street.
The drum beat
grew louder.
And louder.
And louder.

Mary looked
up the street
as hard as she could.
She could see
nothing but the street.
The drum beat
was very loud now.
People came out
of their homes.
The street
filled with people.

Everyone watched
as a row of heads
showed up
at the top of the hill.
The row of heads
became rows of men.
The men
marched down the street.
One of them
beat a drum.
They were tired and dirty.
Some walked
on one leg
with crutches.

Mary ran
up the street.
She looked
until she could see
every man's face.
She looked
at each one
as the front row
came nearer and nearer.
She saw faces
that she knew
from before the war.

Where was Johnny?
Where was the face
she loved the most?

Then a man
in the front row
waved his hand.
"Mary!"
he called.

Mary's heart
skipped a beat.
The man
did not look like Johnny.
This man
had long hair
and a beard.
His clothes
were rags.

"Mary!"
he called again.

"Johnny!"
called Mary.
"Of course,
it is you!

Of course,
you came home!
Of course,
you are walking
right up front!"

"Yes, I am!"
came the voice
she knew so well.
"I am home!"

Johnny's voice
sounded weak.
He looked thin,
His arm
was hurt.
But he was
in one piece.
And he was home.
Johnny McGee
had come marching home.

The North
had won the war.
The Irish Brigade
had helped.

Boston threw
a big party.

Thousands of people
gathered in the streets.
A band played.
Everyone sang along.
Everyone moved
back and forth
like ocean waves.

"What will you do now?"
Mary asked Johnny.

"When I am strong again,
I want to run
for city office,"
said Johnny.
"I want
to help run this city.

And so he did.
Johnny McGee
became a big name
in Boston.
Mary left the Brocks
and took care
of her own family.
Every night
she cooked
a hot dinner.

Almost always,
there were potatoes
in the pot.

Johnny and Mary
did not get old.
Their bodies
wore out
from hard work.
But they died happy,
not hungry.
And their new country
was better and stronger
because of them.

Their children –
John and Patrick and Bridget
and the others –
lived better lives
than Johnny and Mary
had lived.
In their homes,
almost every night,
there were potatoes
for dinner.

Glossary

Definitions and examples of certain words and terms used in the story

Chapter 1 — **The Old Days** page 1

lap — When a person sits, it is the space formed on top of the legs. Children and pets can sit there.
She was holding her son Little John on her lap.

boil — To cook something by heating it in very hot water.
Boil a few potatoes in a big pot over the fire, and that is dinner!

carried on (to carry on) — To continue talking, especially while telling a story.
And Father Patrick carried on.

Chapter 2 — **Potato Problems** page 5

sprouts — A plant as it first appears on the surface of the ground.
Before long, green potato sprouts popped up.

blight — A plant disease.
rotting (to rot) — To change from being
a healthy plant to becoming an
unusable dying plant.
I hear it's a blight. The plants are rotting!

crop — An entire planting of an
agricultural product.
The potato crop could fail!

get by — To survive with some difficulty.
"We can get by," said Mary.

get through — To survive with difficulty
over a period of time.
We can get through one bad year.

pretended (to pretend) — To look like
something is true, when it is not.
They pretended to eat with him.

weeds — Plants that are usually not useful.
They ate weeds.

fall back on — To have and use an extra
supply of something in reserve.
We have no old potatoes to fall back on!

starved (to starve) — To die from not
having food.
People starved to death.

Chapter 3 — **Leaving Ireland** page 12

saw them off (to see someone off) —
To go with someone to their departure.
Father Patrick saw them off.

blessing — A kind of prayer given as an
approval.
"You have my blessing"

hugged (to hug) — to hold someone close to
the body for a moment.
He hugged each one.

coin toss — A coin is thrown up in the air, and
a decision is made on the basis of how it lands
— "heads or tails."
Kennedy lost a coin toss.

set foot — to arrive.
The McGees set foot in America.

Chapter 4 — **Greenhorns in America** page 16

greenhorn — A name for people who are
inexperienced at something. Often they can
be tricked.
"I'm here to help you greenhorns."

Chapter 5 — Hard Work page 22

pick — A tool with a sharp metal point used to break up rock.

shovel — A tool like a spoon used for picking up broken rock and earth.
Johnny was given a pick and a shovel.

spikes — Large nails used to hold things together. Usually pounded by a hammer.
He drove spikes into the rails.

blasting (to blast) — Using explosives to break rock into small pieces.
Blasting large rocks was the worst work of all.

get blown up — To be destroyed by explosives.
More than once, he saw his friends get blown up along with the rocks.

spun (to spin) — A process by which a machine turns very fast and makes cloth.
The machine spun wool.

Chapter 6 — **Blasting Rock** page 27

drilled (to drill) — To use a tool that makes holes in things. In this case, rock.
The men drilled holes into the rock.

right-hand man — A most important assistant.
Murphy became Johnny's right-hand man.

count on — To depend on, to be always helpful.
Johnny knew he could count on Murphy.

fuse — Something that will cause an explosion.
He stuck a fuse, or cord, into the black powder.

packed down (to pack down) — To push down on the ground to make it firm.
pole — A long stick.
He packed down the sand with an iron pole.

spark — A tiny, very hot piece of metal or wood that can cause an explosion or a fire.
set off — To cause something to suddenly become active.
It made a spark that set off the black powder.

Chapter 7 — **Boston Life** page 32

shack — A very small house, usually not
well-made.
board — Long, narrow piece of wood.
*Some families lived in tiny shacks made
of old boards.*

run-down — (A building) that needs repair, in
bad shape.
. . . one small room in a run-down building.

tub — A large container used for washing
clothes and bodies.
*In the room there were two chairs, a black
stove, and an iron tub.*

played by the rules — to live socially
acceptable lives.
*He and Mary went to mass every Sunday.
They played by the rules.*

went off (to go off) — To make a sound.
*When the bell went off, Johnny took his
coat off the hook and ran.*

ward heeler — A worker for a political
machine.
"You should become a ward heeler."

Chapter 8 — The Church page 39

broke out (to break out) — To start.
break them up — Used with "fight," means to
stop the fighters.
*Fights broke out. The police had to break
them up.*

nickname — An informal, often affectionate
name, commonly the short form of a formal
name; Thomas' nickname was Tom or Tommy.
"Biddy was Bridget's nickname."

set off sparks — To cause or start something
that will become a "hot" problem.
*"Let it be," said Johnny. "We don't want
to set off sparks."*

mob — A group of angry, even dangerous
people.
stormed (to storm) — To move angrily
and quickly.
Suddenly a mob of men stormed into the yard.

gravestone — A stone marking the place
where someone is buried.
*The children hid behind the gravestones
in the yard.*

Chapter 9 — Going to War page 44

volunteer unit — A group of people who offer
their time, money, or even life for a cause.
Johnny helped put together a volunteer unit.

brigade — A large military unit, usually
between two and three thousand   soldiers.
*They joined the Irish Brigade and marched off
to war.*

Chapter 10 — No Irish Need Apply page 48

in charge — Leading and directing others.
*The older children helped with the younger ones.
But Mary was in charge.*

slammed (to slam) — To close or shut something
quickly and loudly.
She slammed the door on her way out.

Chapter 12 — News page 56

give up — To stop trying to do something.
a matter of time — It won't continue and will end
at some time.
"They will give up. It's a matter of time."

rag — A piece of cloth used for cleaning.
She heard his name in every push of the rag.

Chapter 13 — **War Is Over**   page 60

showed up (to show up) — To appear, become
 visible.
 *Everyone watched as a row of heads showed up
 at the top of the hill.*

crutches — a (usually) wooden device held
 under the arms to assist with walking.
 Some walked on one leg with crutches.

skipped (to skip) a beat — To be suddenly
 surprised, as if the heart stopped for a second.
 Mary's heart skipped a beat.

wore out (to wear out) — To die or become
 useless because of too much use or hard work.
 Their bodies wore out from hard work.

The Hopes and Dreams Series
by Tana Reiff

The Magic Paper (Mexican-Americans)
For Gold and Blood (Chinese-Americans)
Nobody Knows (African-Americans)
Little Italy (Italian-Americans)
Hungry No More (Irish-Americans)
Sent Away (Japanese-Americans)
Two Hearts (Greek-Americans)

ProLinguaAssociates.com